B40

# Paperwhite

*To Cyd and Bobbi, Claudia, Robin and Sally;*
*to Doe, Judy, Kay, Leslie C., Leslie B., Lorraine and Mary Kelly;*
*and to Amy—*
*thank you for nurturing this book and me.*
*with love, N.E.W.*

# Paperwhite

*Written and illustrated by* Nancy Elizabeth Wallace

Houghton Mifflin Company
Boston 2000

On the first day of winter, Lucy looked out her window and saw Miss Mamie gathering something.
She ran next door to help. They filled a tin pail with small stones and went inside.

"Now," said Miss Mamie, "let's bring a little spring into this dark winter day."

Gently they put the stones into a big glass jar.
Ching. Ching. Ching. Ching.

Lucy covered the stones with water.

Then Miss Mamie handed her a bag
with a small brown lump in it.
"It's a paperwhite bulb," she explained.

Lucy laid the shiny bulb on the pebble nest.
She was very careful not to bump the tender shoots.

Days passed.

The winter days grew longer while winter nights grew shorter.

Lucy knocked on her neighbor's door.

"Miss Mamie, did it grow yet? Did we make spring?"

Lucy ran inside to see.
She added water to the jar to keep the roots wet.

Then Miss Mamie and Lucy mixed cookie dough
and cut out shapes.

Days passed.

The winter days grew even longer and lighter.

Lucy came back to see Miss Mamie.

She poured more water into their jar.

Together they made music.
Miss Mamie played the bottom notes
while Lucy played the top ones.

Days passed.

The winter days grew longer and brighter still!

They checked the jar.

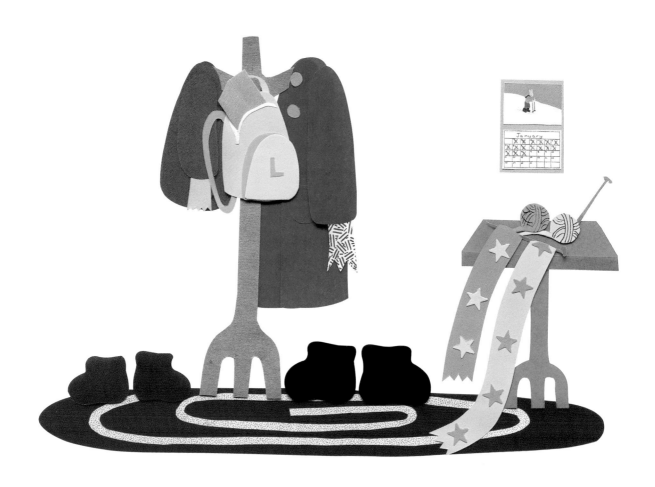

Then Lucy got her bead box.
She and Miss Mamie threaded beads
on thick black string.

The next time Lucy came to visit,
a sweet fragrance filled the air.

"Miss Mamie, we made spring!"

The text of this book is set in 18-point Goudy.
The illustrations were created using scissors, a glue stick, tape, tweezers, and origami and found paper.

*Library of Congress Cataloging-in-Publication Data*

Wallace, Nancy Elizabeth.
Paperwhite / written and illustrated by Nancy Elizabeth Wallace.
p.   cm.
Summary: Lucy and Miss Mamie while away the long hours of winter in various ways while waiting
for a paperwhite bulb to grow and bring them spring.
ISBN 0-618-04283-0
[1. Winter — Fiction.  2. Spring — Fiction.]   I. Title.
PZ7.W15875 Pap   2000
[E] — dc21
99-089178

Printed in Singapore
TWP 10 9 8 7 6 5 4 3 2 1